OHIO READING CIRCLE BOOK
Grade 6
1980-81

MISTER WOLF AND ME

Books by Mary Francis Shura

Mister Wolf and Me
The Gray Ghosts of Taylor Ridge
The Riddle of Ravens' Gulch

MISTER WOLF AND ME

MARY FRANCIS SHURA

Illustrated by Konrad Hack

Dodd, Mead & Company
New York

*All the characters in this story
are fictional with the exception
of Mister Wolf himself whose name
in real life was Guspodin Volkov.*

Library of Congress Cataloging in Publication Data

Shura, Mary Francis.
    Mister Wolf and me.

    SUMMARY: Thirteen-year-old Miles desperately
tries to prove his German shepherd has not been
killing a farmer's sheep.
    [1. Dogs—Fiction] I. Hack, Konrad.
II. Title.
PZ7.S55983Mi   [Fic]   78–22432
ISBN 0–396–07666–1

To Ngaire with love

Contents

Chapter One

JORDAN AGGERS

THE FIRST TIME I ever saw Jordan Aggers I hoped I would never see him again.

It happened at the general store in early August. I had ridden down there with my dog, Mister Wolf, loping along beside my bike. I guessed he was about six months old then but big for his age and the best-looking German shepherd that anyone in this town has seen.

The man who runs the obedience school had told me to wait for the fall session to start Mister Wolf because he was so young, but I think he was wrong. Mister Wolf was really eager to learn. Already he had learned to sit and stay, even though he'd tremble a lot when I went on without him.

After I parked my bike and fastened Mister Wolf's leash to it, I told him to stay until I got back.

I wasn't in that store more than five minutes. When I came out this strange young man in jeans and a funny, painted shirt was standing over my dog. I noticed that faded blue pickup truck that Mr. Aggers always drove there at the curb but I didn't put the two things together right then.

When you are thirteen and not all that big for your age, you don't challenge guys in their twenties, as this fellow looked to be. I just stood there and waited for his frowning inspection of my dog to be over.

He glanced up at me right away and his tone of voice was blunt and really unfriendly. "Where did you get that dog?"

He couldn't have asked a harder question. I found Mister Wolf and brought him home from the woods when he was barely weaned. He sure slurped a lot when he drank out of a saucer, he was that much of a baby.

It had been early May when I found him, and it was still really wet in the woods. I was

10

following a little stream that had a sort of embankment on one side that was higher than my head. When I first heard the whimpering sound I stopped dead still, afraid there was something up there that might jump on me.

Then I realized the sound was coming from around the bend and I speeded up to see what it was. There was a puppy kind of marooned up on a broad flat rock. He cried as if he were calling someone but there was no sign of any other animal in sight.

For a long time after I kept dreading that someone would try to claim him. Even Dad had frowned thoughtfully when I brought him home.

"It's hard to believe that anyone would abandon a well-marked shepherd like that," he told me. "He must have wandered off from home."

"But there was nobody there," I argued. "And it was clear up in the wild part where there aren't any houses for miles."

Mom looked thoughtful. "If it was any-where near the river, he might have wan-dered off from a fishing camp. A lot of fami-lies go there on weekends when the fish start to bite in the spring."

Dad nodded in agreement. "Whoever lost him is bound to make some effort to get back a nice pup like that. You'll have to watch the ads before you can feel free to keep him," he said. "And don't make the mistake of getting your hopes up."

I did watch the ads but my hopes rose anyway. After a month or so passed I quit watching ads, because Mister Wolf was mine and I had raised him. And here this guy comes out of nowhere asking me where I got him. A cold hard lump came in my stomach at his question.

"I've had him a long time," I said, not wanting to make up some fancy lie that I might get caught in later.

The skin around the guy's eyes tightened and he really stared at me. In fact, you might say he glared at me in a kind of know-it-all way, looking me up and down, at my clothes and my new sneakers that hadn't even been washed yet, and at my ten-speed that my folks had given me for my last birthday. I was suddenly conscious that everything about me looked awfully new and expensive next to his jeans, which had dark patches and the bottoms frayed off, and his boots that had something rough on the toes where the leather had been.

"Don't play any games with me, kid," he said curtly. "I didn't ask how long you'd had him. I asked you where you got him."

It was my good luck that Dad's friend Mr. Austen, who sells real estate and is in and out of the general store all the time, happened to step outside and hear his tone of voice. Mr. Austen looked over at us curiously and then walked over.

"Something the matter here, Miles?" he asked.

Usually I don't care much for the way the people in this town wear themselves out minding other people's business, but right then I liked it.

"I don't think so," I replied with some hesitation. "This man just asked me where I got my dog."

"Do you have some reason to think that Miles doesn't have a right to his dog?" Mr. Austen asked in this very cool voice.

The young man flushed and stiffened at Mr. Austen's question. "I just asked him where he got the animal," he said firmly. "It's pretty funny that he can't give a straight answer to a simple question like that."

"Maybe he figures that it is none of your business," Mr. Austen told him. "That would be my first thought if I were he."

The young man glared at him and then at me and then at Mister Wolf for a long minute. Naturally Mister Wolf thought this was the greatest ever. He sat up as straight as he could so as not to miss any of the attention. He was grinning the way shepherds do, with his tongue hanging halfway down his chest and his tail thumping a steady rhythm on the sidewalk so hard that you'd have thought it would hurt.

Then the young man pivoted on his heel and walked off fast as if he were really angry. Mr. Austen and I watched him climb into that old blue pickup that Mr. Aggers had had since I can remember. The truck backfired a couple of times and went up north on Main, leaving a trail of dark smoke behind it.

Mr. Austen shook his head as he watched the truck leave. "That boy doesn't fit in any better around here than he did when he was growing up."

"I never saw him before," I said, feeling

the hard lump in my stomach starting to go away a little.

"He's Jordan Aggers, old Jim Aggers' boy," Mr. Austen told me. "He and his dad never did get along much and he took off from home when he was still a kid. I don't think he even finished high school. But he came back here last winter when his dad died and has been living out there ever since."

"Alone?" I asked, thinking of what a scary place that Aggers farm would be at night.

He shook his head. "I guess his mother is there too. She has been in poor health for years and almost never gets into town, but as far as I know she's still out there."

I biked home slowly to give Mister Wolf a chance to do all his exploring along the roadside. I was exploring myself, trying to figure out in my own mind why this Jordan Aggers was so curious about Mister Wolf. I guess I had heard that old Mr. Aggers had died but I don't pay that much attention to grown-up talk. I did remember Mr. Aggers and that blue truck of his well enough. He was a short-legged, heavyset sort of man with a closed-in looking face and white hair trimmed really close so that his scalp looked pink underneath.

I didn't really know whether I'd been afraid of Mr. Aggers because of the way he looked so cross all the time or because he lived where he did. The Aggers farm is out northwest of town just off the road where the post used to run in the old days. There are always a lot of stories about post roads, and that stretch along there has had the name of being haunted ever since Revolutionary War days. They say that a drummer boy was robbed and killed there and the echo of his drum sounds along the road on certain nights, a muffled, ghostly cadence that warns the hearer that something ugly is going to happen to him.

But the hill where I found Mister Wolf is clear off in the opposite direction. There was no way that he could have been Jordan Aggers' dog and wandered off that far.

It is always mysterious where strange dogs come from anyway. Sometimes they stray off from fishermen's camps and get lost in the woods. Sometimes people even dump them along the road because they don't want them any more. But the dogs always seem to find each other. They form wild packs that live up in the hills like wild animals. We can hear them at night from our place when the windows are open. They range in a big pack and attack the stock on the outlying farms. The sound of their howling makes the hair rise up on your arms something awful.

From the way Mister Wolf acted that first day I found him, he had never seen a human being before. He snarled and tried to get me with those baby teeth like a real wolf. There was just no way a puppy that small could have gotten from the Aggers' place to where I found him.

But it worried me a long time that Jordan Aggers had asked that question the way he did.

Chapter Two

Pᴉɴ Hɪʟʟ

THERE OUGHT TO be some way to tell in advance what kind of a day you're getting into. Maybe mornings should come marked like medicine bottles. If a nice straight manageable day was coming, the sky could be free and cloudless. But if you were headed into a really murderous time, a small tasteful skull and crossbones could form in dark clouds to give you warning.

That October Thursday was poison if I ever had it.

And in defense of my own instincts, I must have been getting some signs and omens because I had put that nut-gathering trip off as long as I could. But it was Thursday that

Mom got her head set on "go" and she managed to get Mister Wolf and me tangled up with that Jordan Aggers again.

There is only one week in the fall when it is worth anyone's time to go gathering hickory nuts. If you go too early you can shake those limbs until your teeth get loose but the nuts stay on like they were glued. If you wait one week too late, an army of squirrels will have marched through the clearing leaving empty, curled nut hulls shoe-top deep and not a nut for miles.

On Monday afternoon Mom had said, "I bet that last night's frost brought the hickory nuts down."

That was a hint.

I told her about the two extra pages of math that Mr. Elroy had assigned us after the spitball fight that I didn't start but got blamed for, because when I shot back at Matt Turpin he ducked and I hit Mr. Elroy on the left cheek.

Tuesday after school she said, "If you're going after hickory nuts you'd better leave right away because the days are sure getting shorter."

That was a suggestion. I showed her the

map of the township that I had to have colored in with all the place names marked by first period if I wanted a social studies grade. She pursed her lips that prim way but didn't press it.

Wednesday she pointed out that if I went all winter without nuts in Saturday night fudge I wasn't to blame anyone but myself.

That was a threat and I really considered going. But there was a big dark cloud boiling up in the west and I wondered out loud if she wanted to risk my getting a really rotten cold like I had the spring before. That time I was out of school for almost two weeks and she had to cancel bridge club and a shopping trip and change my linen twice because the medicine made me sick at my stomach.

I wouldn't dare let her hear this but Mom has a really strange head. It's as if she had gears in there that she shifts at will. Most of the time she has her head set on neutral so that her brain just idles. Things flow in and out of her ears without even registering. When she is passing out hints and suggestions you can figure she is still idling. When she gets to the threatening stage you know that the next shift will be into high and you'd better be ready to move on demand.

Thursday afternoon she was waiting at the back door when I got in from school. She handed me a mesh sack and a plastic bag of brownies. "I packed these for you to eat on the way," she said. "Go pick hickory nuts."

Since that was an order, Mister Wolf and I were on our way to Pin Hill before the school bus turned around and started back to town.

It's a good stiff walk to Pin Hill, past the general store and north, with the land rising steadily after you leave the middle of town behind.

After I shared the brownies with Mister Wolf he raced ahead to nose into every clump of grass. We stopped to stare at the cornhusk spooks that people had set out for Hallowe'en. It's fun to see what they dress them in—great stacks of cornhusks with carved pumpkin faces and old work hats pushed down on straw hair. The same frost that Mom was so sure had brought the hickory nuts down had nipped the jack-o'-lanterns too, so that their smiles slumped crookedly and sometimes an eye had fallen into a playful wink.

But I could tell winter was coming from Mister Wolf's coat. His deep silver-and-sable hair had already grown in so thick that I could hardly part it enough to see his skin underneath.

By the time we reached the center of town and Mister Wolf had taken a quick run on that wide green place there on the square that everybody calls the common, it was getting a little chilly. As soon as we started up the hills toward Pin Hill, a really cold little breeze began to whip around us. The trees were blazing with leaf color and the wind carried the scent of wood fires from the chimneys of houses along the road. All of the clearings on Pin Hill look just the same to me so I just kept walking until I found an area where the yellow leaves of nut trees were thick in among the darker colors of pin oak. I never worry about getting lost on Pin Hill because of the way Main Street extends due north of the common along those hills. If I just walk straight east (which I can tell if the sunset is at my back) I will always run into the road and be able to find my way back home.

By the time I found a clearing with plenty

of nuts in it, Mister Wolf was long gone on his own dog business. I could tell the direction he had taken by the insulted shrieks of jays and the chatter of squirrels telling him off from safe high limbs.

When I had the sack about a third full, he came back to check on me, his tongue hanging out of the side of his mouth and that mischievous smile on his face. I went on crawling in the fallen leaves and scooping nuts into my sack while he went scouting off again.

When he first started to bark I didn't pay any attention. I figured he might have flushed some rabbits or have a particularly irritating squirrel treed. I did notice that his barking went on a long time and was very steady. When it changed to a low growl, I straightened up and yelled for him to come. That was when I heard the unmistakable sounds of snapping and yelping that meant a fight.

I ran, yelling and whistling, but the sounds only got louder. I had dropped my nut bag in the clearing, and I ran as fast as I could with the low branches lashing at me as I passed.

When I broke through the last line of trees, the whole floor of the clearing was a mass of rolling, snarling fur. Mister Wolf was locked in battle with what I thought at first was a small fat dog. But then as they rolled toward me I saw the face of the meanest-looking groundhog ever. He was fat as a custard and he was raking at Mister Wolf with old ugly fangs while he hung on with his long claws buried in Mister Wolf's skin.

Mister Wolf was much bigger and out-weighed the groundhog by a whole lot, but the old animal was a far more skilled fighter. I kept shouting while I looked around for a stick to separate them. The first one I found was old and dead and splintered into nothing when I put my weight on it.

It seemed like forever before I finally got the strong branch I needed and went back to the clearing. All the stories I have ever heard about groundhogs flashed through my mind, about dogs they had torn up so badly that the dogs had to be put to sleep. And even if it survived, a dog could lose an eye or be crippled for life by one of those varmints.

At first it didn't seem that I was even

going to be able to separate them with the stick. They rolled and wrestled so fast and so ferociously that every time I thought I had a clear aim on the groundhog, he rolled away and I came within an ace of bashing my own dog.

Finally I got my chance by just dancing around them with the stick poised in the air like a Japanese dancer or something. When I saw an opening, I plunged the stick between their bodies, bringing it down hard so that the groundhog, still holding a lot of Mister Wolf's skin in his paws, was tossed loose and rolled a few feet away.

I shouted at Mister Wolf to stay and went after the groundhog. That woodchuck was so full of fight that he wasn't even thinking about getting away. Instead he was facing me, his teeth bared and his claws up. I brought the stick down on his head hard and something turned in my stomach at the sound of the wood hitting his skull. But the claws went limp and he went down in a reddish-brown mound there among the leaves.

Mister Wolf was straining at my command, itching to get back into the fight, apparently not realizing that patches of his skin were hanging loose and he was bleeding a lot from some cuts around his throat and head.

When I knelt by him I could feel him tremble, and the way he was bleeding really scared me. I laid my hand on his back and felt the hair as stiff as the bristles on a barbecue brush.

I had to get help and fast but I couldn't remember seeing a house for miles. I thought right off about Doc Fletcher. Mom hates it when I call him that because she thinks it sounds disrespectful, but I know Doc himself doesn't mind. Ever since Mister Wolf was a pup I had always taken him there to the office by the common for shots and things. I always forget to say that whole Doctor thing and he never even looks up at me.

"Come on, fellow, you'll have to walk," I told Mister Wolf.

He whimpered when I took his collar and started leading him away. He kept looking back at the clearing and making small feints as if he still meant to break away from me and fight some more.

"It's going to hurt more if I have to drag you," I told him, tugging at his collar. He whimpered again at the pressure and started along, only looking back every few minutes with a low growl of warning.

It didn't seem to me that the groundhog was going to threaten anyone ever again. From the way he lay there in that thick silent ball, I figured that I had killed him.

Keeping the streaks of sunset color at my back I tugged and coaxed Mister Wolf through what seemed like miles of woods, over stone fences I had never seen, even across one country lane where I hesitated a minute hoping there would be a house in sight. Nothing.

When it seemed that dark was going to overtake us and that we were never going to get anywhere, I heard the sound of a car passing and knew we had finally reached the road.

A barbed-wire fence ran along the ridge there above the road and I couldn't hang onto Mister Wolf and get us both through it at the same time. When I got the strands pressed apart to make room enough for Mister Wolf, he almost wouldn't go without me.

Finally I shoved him with my knee and he went through and down the incline. I was still trying to get a barb loose from my coat when I heard the car coming. "Get back," I shouted, but Mister Wolf was just standing there dazed at the edge of the road.

The car was coming fast. Then the driver must have caught the dog in his headlights. The car slowed down. I tried to shout for the driver to stop but the sight of Mister Wolf, his eyes wide into the blaze of light and the bloody flaps of fur around his neck, must have scared the man. He hit the accelerator hard and was off before I could get down there by my dog.

But at least we were on the north-south road, headed for Main Street and town. Each step seemed to hurt Mister Wolf more than the last. Once in a while he would try to lie down on the side of the road but I kept prodding him up, coaxing him. We had to get to Doc Fletcher's before it was too late for Mister Wolf.

The wind was brisker all the time and for some reason it made painful raw streaks when it whipped across my face.

Chapter Three

Doc Fletcher

THE STREETLIGHTS were just blinking on as Mister Wolf and I finally reached the common. My heart sank. If it was six o'clock already Doc Fletcher would probably be long gone from his office. And not that I could do anything about it right then, but Mom would be watching the windows with fire in her eyes. Mom likes to think of herself as a person of great courage and she is about most things. But when she gets scared, like when Dad or I get sick or she is afraid something has happened to us, she gets mad at us for scaring her. It's worth your life to get really sick around her because she will bite your head off before the disease gets you.

Even though the office lights were off, I took Mister Wolf over to Doc Fletcher's building anyway. Sure enough, there was a room still lit at the back and I could see a figure moving around inside. If there were any sick animals staying at the kennel at the back, maybe the night person was there too and would be able to help Mister Wolf some way. I rapped on the door for a long time before I got any response. Then, to my immense relief, I could see it was Doc Fletcher himself coming through the dark waiting room to unlock the door.

He only opened it a crack at first. "I'm closed for the night, Miles. Come in early tomorrow."

"You got to look at Mister Wolf right away," I pleaded. "He's really hurt!"

He hesitated a minute before widening the crack. "I wouldn't even be here except that my night helper is a little late. I've got to leave on a call out north of town as soon as he comes."

"Just look at him," I pleaded. "He got into a terrible fight and has bled a whole lot."

He opened the door all the way and peered down at Mister Wolf. "Well, in that

34

case . . ." As he spoke he took hold of Mister Wolf's collar and led him toward the light.

"Good Lord," he cried when he got a good look at him. "He really did get torn up. I hope the other dog has had his rabies shot on schedule."

"It wasn't a dog," I explained, squatting beside Mister Wolf to steady him with my hands. "It was a great big groundhog out on Pin Hill."

"A groundhog!" Doc Fletcher turned to me with amazement. "I've heard of them giving a big fight but this is incredible. He must have been one mad varmint to tackle a dog this size. Easy there, fellow," he coaxed. Mister Wolf whimpered once or twice while the doctor cleaned his wounds with some solution that made the inside of my head tingle. Then he slipped a hypodermic in beside the worst torn place on the dog's neck and rubbed the needle site a minute with the flat of his thumb.

I held Mister Wolf still but I didn't look again for a while. I heard the sound of the back door opening just as Doc finished tying off the last stitch in Mister Wolf's neck. Then Doc looked up at me with a reassuring

smile. "How's that for timing? That will be Ed coming to relieve me just when I've done all I can do for this fellow for a while."

He washed his hands and then handed me a small brown envelope. "Give him one of these twice a day. They'll help fight off infection. How big did you say that groundhog was again?"

When I held out my hands to show him, he whistled softly. "He must have been all fight, that fellow."

"They both were," I told him. "And I got really scared."

Mister Wolf had collapsed on the floor and was staring up at me with that betrayed look he always gets when I let someone do something unpleasant to him. Doc Fletcher frowned a little as he looked down at him.

"It would sure be better if you didn't make him walk home. I could drop you off myself except for this call north of town. Is your dad home this week?"

I shook my head. "Not until tomorrow night, but if you'll let me use your phone, Mom will come after us."

"No problem there," he said, pulling his leather jacket off the hook. "Ed will let you out when you're through. And let me see those stitches in about a week."

Mom's voice was pretty shrill when she answered the phone but when I told her where I was she settled down a little. When I told her about the fight on the way home she sighed. "Poor old fellow," she said thoughtfully. "He has probably been guarding that clearing all his life. It's too bad the two of them had to tangle."

"I hated it when I had to hit him," I told her, knowing she would understand how I felt. "I never killed anything warm like that before."

She didn't say anything but I saw her nod in the darkness.

Mister Wolf was getting stiffer by the minute. It took both of us to help him out of the car. "Not that anything can be done about it, but your dinner is probably past saving," she said as she closed the door behind us.

"Since it is Thursday, it probably wasn't worth saving," I replied. That's a kind of private joke between Mom and me. With Dad on the road all week, Mom and I get down to pretty simple meals compared to the spreads she cooks up on weekends.

She giggled the way that reminds me that she must have been thirteen once herself. "Leftovers tonight mean Dad's home tomorrow," she said.

"I guess he won't be calling in tonight," I said, feeling a little wistful about that.

"By the time Dad comes, Mister Wolf will be on the way to his old self," she said with assurance.

Chapter Four

SHERIFF CRAVENS

YOU CAN ALWAYS tell when a stranger is outside our schoolroom. A big rustling starts up at the front of the room and the kids up there start growing giraffe necks that sway back and forth as they strain to peer out through the half glass in the door.

I am usually as nosy as the next guy but when they started peering and straining in math class that Friday I didn't pay any attention.

To be honest, I was having trouble getting my attention on anything but my own thoughts that day. The whole night before had been a long nightmare. Mister Wolf slept on his rug in my room as usual but he whimpered softly every once in a while all night long. I kept getting up to tell him he was going to be all right, and then by the time I settled back to sleep he would be whimpering again. I'm not used to being awake all night and the sounds I heard really spooked me.

I had recognized the cry of the owl after the first time or two but I got tired of his calling to his friend and the low mournful hoot of his friend's reply. The sound of the dog pack howling off in the far woods sent a chill up my spine the way it always does. I've never seen those dogs but I can imagine them with gleaming eyes and wide-open dripping mouths like something out of a horror movie. But somehow the tapping bothered me the most. There was just enough wind so the loose shutter outside the master-bedroom window was tapping a signal once in a while, then stopping and starting again. I kept trying to remember Morse code as if the dots and dashes were giving me some sinister message about Mister Wolf. In spite of Doc Fletcher's reassurances and Mom's optimism, it was hard for me to feel that Mister Wolf was getting along as well as he should be.

Not since that first day that I brought him home from the woods as a puppy had I ever seen him as listless. He hardly tried to raise his head when I spoke to him. He tried to wag his tail but it was almost embarrassing what a bad job he made of it, just a half-hearted little thump and then nothing. He would only open his eyes halfway and they looked glazed as if something hung there between him and me.

Finally I noticed that the giraffe necks up at the front of the room were looking back at me and Matt Turpin was mouthing something and pointing his finger like a recruitment poster. I just shook my head at him. Whatever was in the hall didn't interest me. I just wanted this stupid day to get itself over with so I could go see how Mister Wolf was getting along.

Finally Mr. Elroy went outside to check. When he came back in he motioned me up front.

I knew something terrible was going on when I saw my mom out there still wearing her morning face and standing beside Sheriff Cravens like she was a prisoner or something. Whatever was going on had to be pretty big stuff. Nothing gets my mother out of bed early in the morning. By the time I was in kindergarten I knew better than to say word number one to her at the beginning of a day. My own theory is that her real personality freezes in the night and has to be thawed out with coffee in the morning.

I shut the door behind me quick, halfway hoping I would catch somebody's long nose in it. Then I whispered, "What did you do, Mom?"

From the way her eyes widened and her mouth dropped I knew she was still about three cups of coffee away from being ready for all this.

"What did I do?" she squalled. "What kind of a question is that?"

Sheriff Cravens grew up in this town just like Mom and Dad both did. Maybe he knew her well enough to try to protect her morning self. Anyway he spoke up quickly. "I asked your mom to come down with me, Miles." Then after a furtive glance at her, he went on. "I know it was a big inconvenience but I wanted her along when I came to talk to you."

"But I haven't done anything either," I told him quickly. There is something about the light reflection off the buttons of a law officer's uniform that makes your life flash before your eyes. Every rock I had ever thrown, every moustache I had painted on a candidate's picture, every rotten apple I had ever hidden in a school-bus seat swam before my eyes and I was ready to confess to anything.

"I know that, Miles," he said reassuringly. "I just came over to hear your story of how that German shepherd of yours got all cut up last night."

"I told Mom already," I said, glancing at her. From the closed look on her face I couldn't tell whether she was just staying out of this on principle or because it was still too early in the morning.

So I repeated about going up to Pin Hill for the nuts and about the fight and how Doc Fletcher had sewed Mister Wolf back up.

"And nobody else was there?" he asked.

"I wish there had been," I said. "I really needed help."

Then he stood very still staring at that bulletin board where the school posts all the rules of what you aren't allowed to do.

45

Down at the bottom some comedian had added a handwritten line that read "Breathe in or out." I suddenly realized that I was having a little trouble doing that myself.

"What's all this about Mister Wolf?" I asked, unable to wait any longer without exploding inside.

He shook his head unhappily. "I don't know whether eighth graders read the papers or not but you must have heard about how those wild dog packs have been killing stock all over the country the past few years."

"Mister Wolf is no wild-running dog," I said.

"Well, I hope not," he replied, not meeting my eyes. "But Jordan Aggers had five lambs slaughtered by wild dogs yesterday afternoon late. The guard dog he keeps out there was pretty badly cut up, too. When Doc Fletcher came out to minister to the flock and Aggers' dog, Doc commented to Jordan that he'd sewed up your dog right before he left the office. It seemed pretty much of a coincidence to Jordan."

"It wasn't Mister Wolf that fought his dog

or killed his sheep," I told him. "I was with him all the time."

"Jordan claims he got a good look at the last dog of the pack to leave and he wants to come over and look at your animal."

"Let him come," I said, feeling suddenly relieved. "There isn't a German shepherd anywhere around here that looks like my dog. He'll know right off that he's on the wrong track. I get home from school a little before four if he wants to come and get it over with."

Sheriff Cravens hesitated. "He intimated that he wanted to be sure that your father was there when he came. How about around seven?"

When I nodded, Sheriff Cravens kind of led Mom away while I just stood there.

Jordan Aggers was just trying to be threatening by saying he wanted my dad to be there. He was going to feel pretty silly when he saw Mister Wolf and had to admit he was forty miles wrong about my dog.

Chapter Five

RETURN TO PIN HILL

THAT DAY GOT darker and darker and it wasn't just in my head. The faintly milky sky developed great dark-bottomed thunderheads that drooped and threatened beyond the windows. It was a perfect waste of time for me to stay in school. I kept telling myself that I was stupid to worry. Once that old Jordan Aggers saw Mister Wolf he would have to back right off. There aren't any German shepherds in our town that are even the same color as Mister Wolf. Where they are brown and tan, his hair is a deep glossy black against the silvery light part. But with my luck, the man might be color blind. Then what?

Social studies is my next-to-last class. By the time I got there I was driven to use Mom's trick with my head. I just plain turned my whole brain off because I couldn't stand the sound of it boiling and fuming in there. While Mr. Walters droned on about the Ice Age I sat and stared at the row of township maps he had put up along my side of the room. I knew my own map wouldn't be there because I had put a peanut butter sandwich down on my copy. The big mark it left was transparent looking like stained glass without any color. But some people in the class had done really super jobs of filling the maps in and coloring all the different things. Emily Ann is that kind of person who does so much extra stuff that she forces the regular guys like me right off the bottom of the curve. She had put in the Shaker village and Fruitlands and the common with both churches and the right number of houses. Bare Hill Pond was a pale mirror with ducks on it, and Pin Hill was sprinkled with spots of gold like the color of the nut trees the day Mister Wolf and I went up there.

Seeing Pin Hill right there on the map

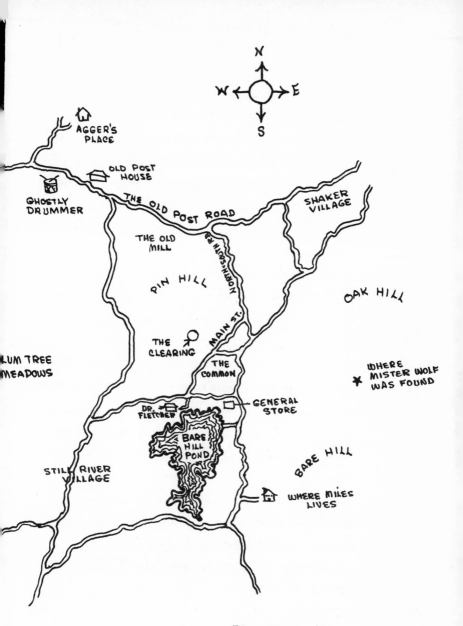

THE TOWNSHIP

brought me my great idea with such a jolt that I nearly jumped out of my chair. The groundhog. I didn't even have to wait for that Jordan Aggers to come over to clear Mister Wolf. That groundhog would be lying out there in that clearing still. If Sheriff Cravens just went out with me and we found it right there where I said it was, he could see for himself how Mister Wolf got so torn up.

Somebody nudged me or I never would have known that Mr. Walters was speaking to me in that tone of his that would take rust off a bike fender.

"Unless you are planning to stay after school and entertain me for thirty minutes of detention, I would suggest you stop bouncing up and down in your seat."

"Yes," I told him. "No, sir, I mean. I'll be still."

He watched me silently a minute before starting in again on what happened to a land mass when a glacier moved over it. And like the motion of a glacier over a land mass, the period finally got through and then the next and I was free.

When I got home I made Mister Wolf get up and walk the length of the driveway and back with me. He obviously did it only to please me but I still felt he ought to move around more and not just lie there like he was trying to die. His tail and his ears all hung down as if they had weights on them and he kind of flopped his feet along at every step. I couldn't even get him to drink any water after I took him back in.

"I guess you filled his food dish again?" I asked Mom hopefully. It didn't look as if what I had put in it that morning had even been touched.

She shook her head. "He'll eat when he feels like it," she said placidly.

Great wisdom like that should be cut in stone, I thought angrily, repeating her words to myself. *He'll eat when he feels like it.* Oh, boy. Dogs die when they don't eat, just like people do. Already the great cave of Mister Wolf's lungs was striped with rib marks where his bones were sticking out. When he wouldn't even sniff at a dog biscuit, I laid it on the floor near his nose in case he changed his mind after I left.

"I have an errand downtown," I told her.

"You might get caught in a rain." (Hint)

It suddenly occurred to me that if I wanted to get out to Pin Hill to check for that groundhog I needed to get Mom stalled before she got her head shifted into high.

"I'll take a raincoat just in case," I offered pleasantly.

Her eyes widened in surprise. She knows I never take a raincoat anywhere except under pain of death. In spite of her astonishment she decided to press her luck. "And boots?" she added. (Suggestion.)

I nodded and went right to the closet where we keep the heavy-weather gear. By the time I got the boots pulled on and the raincoat out she was humming an aimless little tune to herself. I hid my grin. It didn't even matter to me that she thought she had won that round. The important thing was to get to Sheriff Cravens and persuade him to go out and look for the groundhog.

I hate getting the gears on my ten-speed wet but I had spent too much time with Mister Wolf to have any extra minutes for walking down to the sheriff's office. The rain was already spattering as I reached the common and I was actually glad of the raincoat by the time I pushed open the door to the sheriff's office.

He was on the phone when I came in but

he motioned me to a chair and waggled his eyebrows at me. The voice coming from the phone in his hand sounded, from where I sat, like a country music record being played at the wrong speed. Every once in a while he would murmur, "Yes," and the sound would slacken a bit. By the time the squawk had settled into a medium range, he was nodding soothingly.

"That would be very big of you," he said finally. "Give it another week and then check back with me." Then, "I knew you would, Mr. Perkins, and I appreciate it. I really do."

I had to grin because I had figured out what was going on. Everybody in town knows that Joshua Perkins and his brother-in-law, who own houses next door to each other on Stowe Road, are always getting into fights. Between fights, they play checkers together and go fishing and drive over to Concord for dinner. But when they have an argument, one always ends up calling the law out for the other.

It's like a small world in itself, our town, I decided. Like the day that Mr. Austen, Dad's friend, had stepped in when Jordan

Aggers was asking me hard questions about Mister Wolf. He not only knew Jordan Aggers but had made some reference to what kind of a boy he had been. It scared me a little, but it was reassuring too, as if the whole town was a larger extension of our own family.

"Surely you didn't come down here in the rain just to stare at me," Sheriff Cravens said.

I shook my head and shot to my feet. "No, sir, I had a great idea," I told him.

"*You* had an idea. Let *me* decide how great it is," he corrected me with a grin.

"Don't you think that if we went out to that clearing and got that big groundhog that we might be able to convince Jordan Aggers that he's making a mistake in accusing Mister Wolf?"

The sheriff looked thoughtful and then glanced at the window. "Might be," he said. "But I think it would be a better idea if we waited until tomorrow when it may not be raining cats out there."

"But if we wait until tomorrow the buzzards might carry him away or something."

He rose and tugged his jacket off the peg.

"Are you telling me that buzzards take Fridays off and go back to work on Saturdays?"

Before I could answer, he had his jacket zipped and was holding the door open for me. "I need to be back in about an hour when the local citizens start backing their cars into each other to celebrate the coming weekend. Can you lead me right to the place?"

"It's on Pin Hill," I said.

"It is twenty miles from one end of Pin Hill to the other," he pointed out.

"It's close," I assured him. "Where those hickories are, at the very south end."

He nodded approval and asked, "How did you get down here?"

"My bike," I told him.

"We'll go in my car," he said. "But, for goodness sake, lock that bike up tight. I can't even keep track of my own coffee cup in this place. There's no telling what would happen to your bike."

It was raining steadily by the time that we pulled off the road up by Pin Hill. I stood near the car staring into the woods while the sheriff struggled into a giant green rubber poncho.

"This way," I said, starting through the trees as if I was really sure of where I was going, which I most certainly was not.

Suddenly all of Pin Hill looked different to me. The rain darkened everything so that even that special yellow of the hickory leaves didn't show much. In the day since I had been there, the wind had tugged a lot of the leaves off so that the woods looked naked and bare, showing the great untidy squirrels' nests lodged almost dangerously above our heads as we pushed our way through the trees.

The first two clearings I chose were wrong. I got edgier every time I saw Sheriff Cravens sneak a peek at his watch.

Just when I was feeling really panicky I saw, in the clearing ahead, the stick I had used to force the two fighting animals apart. I ran to it with a yelp. "Here it is. This is it," I called out.

I expected to find that great lump of reddish brown animal lying there by the stump where I had last seen it. Instead the clearing was empty, except for that big heavy stick of mine.

"Where's the varmint?" Sheriff Cravens

asked, looking around the clearing.

"Maybe I didn't kill him all the way dead. Maybe something has already carried him off." I felt suddenly desperate. "But look, you can see there was a fight here."

It was true. The bushes were all crushed down and the grass matted over. There were even some watery dark stains of dried blood on the carpet of leaves on the forest floor.

Sheriff Cravens studied the scene carefully and then nodded. "Something happened in this clearing," he said. "That's plain enough. But without the groundhog I don't know how much we can make of it. Aggers is ready to make a federal case out of those lambs of his, and I don't much blame him since it's the only source of income on that farm of his mom's. He isn't going to be easy to convince of anything."

"But it's the truth," I wailed.

"Jordan Aggers is equally sure that what he knows is the truth too," he reminded me.

Something inside me wilted. I felt heavy with discouragement. I turned and started back toward the car. I thought the sheriff was right behind me but when I got there,

I looked around and saw he had gone back into the woods a little farther and was putting something inside the big green poncho he wore. Maybe a handful of nuts, I thought drearily. At least he won't have wasted the whole trip out here.

"What happens when both sides of an argument are sure they have the truth on their side?" I asked when we were both inside the car.

The sheriff flicked on the heater. The air steamed from our wet clothing as he pulled the car back onto the road to town.

"In court it is called a trial," he said mildly. "Between countries it's called a war."

Chapter Six

THE SHADOW OF A DOUBT

IT WAS REALLY dark and far too late by the time I fought my bike back from the sheriff's office and up the hill through the rain to home. Even without seeing Dad's car parked in the driveway I would have known it was Friday night from the good smell pouring out of that kitchen. It was an Italian smell but I couldn't tell exactly what.

"Let me guess, let me guess," I said to Mom as I shut the door behind me and hopped onto the rug to drip.

" 'Let me guess, let me guess,' " she mimicked crossly, turning to glare at me. "You had an innocent errand downtown and were coming home at a decent time but you were kidnapped by a flying saucer . . ."

"It wasn't a saucer at all," I corrected her, trying to keep my face serious. "It was a flying Ark, just like Noah's except that the man in it was green with a long white beard. He bowed very low as he captured me. He warned me that as the waters rose to cover the earth, he had been sent to save the pure of heart and the children of really super cooks like you."

"Then I guess I am lucky to see you at all," she said soberly.

"He smelled that Italian sauce and sent me home for my last meal," I told her, still breathing in that great smell of cheese and spice.

"It's lasagna," she said in a resigned tone, but I could see the grin twitching at the corners of her lips. "You are driving me into an early grave with your late hours and your smart mouth."

"You will have it dug on a high hill, I hope," I called back from the closet. Then I remembered. "Did you say anything to Dad about Mister Wolf and that dumb sheep farmer?"

She hesitated before replying. "I thought we might let him catch his breath from that long drive home."

In a way I was relieved. Then again, I wished she had already told Dad so I wouldn't have to.

When my stuff was all hung up I went to the back room where we keep Mister Wolf's rug behind Dad's big lounge chair. Mom says the chair is too hideous to have out in the living room, where Dad could really enjoy it.

Mister Wolf looked like a mass of dark fur in the shadow of the recliner. "How about it, fellow?" I whispered right down in his face. "Feeling better yet?"

He raised his head a little and I saw the gleam of white teeth. His breath against my face felt extra hot and smelled awful. Then I heard the reassuring drumming of his tail against the rug and he lifted one paw to shake hands.

I could tell that Dad had his breath back from his long drive home when I heard him come pounding down the stairs singing that song about caissons going rolling along. He always sings military songs when he feels good.

"If you two want to sit down, I'll get dinner on the table," Mom called to him. "Come on, Miles."

"Where is that kid, anyway?" Dad grinned at me as I slid into my chair. "Let's hear about all the spectacular grades you made this week while I was gone."

"Perhaps you shouldn't encourage him to exaggerate," Mom said slyly, trying to cut the lasagna into big squares. Great looping strands of melted cheese kept hanging from her knife, and the smell was to die over.

I had lifted the first bite onto my fork to cool when the chimes from the front door sounded. Mom and I both jumped and she got up so awkwardly that her knife clattered to the floor.

Dad stared at the door she had gone through and back at me. "What's up? Were you two expecting someone?"

I nodded. "We meant to tell you first," I began. Then I didn't know what to say. "Mister Wolf, he . . ."

When I paused Dad leaned forward with

concern. "Nothing has happened to him, has it, Son?"

I just shook my head, not knowing how to answer.

At the rumble of men's voices from the living room, Dad laid his napkin aside and got up. He waited while I dragged to my feet and then, without even knowing what was going on, laid his arm across my shoulders as we went into the front room.

Jordan Aggers looked more than a little out of place in Mom's neat living room. His clothes seemed even shabbier when they were wet. He had folded some sort of jacket into his hands but he had been hatless and the rain trickled down from the ends of his hair. Standing there by Sheriff Cravens, he didn't look anything like as big and threatening as he had looked to me that day out in front of the general store.

When Dad and the sheriff had shaken hands, Sheriff Cravens started to introduce Jordan Aggers. Dad shook his head and didn't let him finish. Instead he reached out and took the young man's hand in a hearty handshake.

"I've known Jordan since he was a pup. How are you, son? And how is your ma getting along by now?"

"Maybe a little better," Jordan Aggers replied as if he had been caught off guard by Dad's tone.

"And you're back here now, running the farm for her?" Dad asked.

The young man's face twisted. "I'm trying to." He glanced at me with that cross look. "Dad didn't leave the affairs in very good shape. I'm trying to get Ma squared away with some income from that farm."

Dad waved the two men to chairs while Mom kind of faded off into the kitchen to give some first aid to dinner. "I haven't been cued in yet," Dad said to Sheriff Cravens. "Miles said there was something about his dog."

Young Aggers looked at the sheriff silently and the sheriff squirmed in his chair. He was having as much trouble knowing how to start as I had back there at the table.

"Jordan here has been having a lot of trouble with dogs killing off his sheep," the sheriff began.

Dad shook his head. "That same old prob-

68

lem. We've fought those roving wild dogs for years now, only to have people dump more strays and start it up again. But that can't have anything to do with Mister Wolf."

Jordan was twisting his hands in the jacket on his lap. He looked scared and nervous. I would have felt sorry for him only I felt scared and nervous too, and I wanted the whole thing over so he would go away.

"Just let me tell you what's been going on," Jordan Aggers began. "All this started during the first lambing after my father was buried. The dogs hit the flock and killed two lambs and wounded one of the ewes bad. I put up bright outside lights and tightened the fence with double barbed wire strung around the top. When I lost another lamb just about a week later I took to standing guard.

"It was sometime in late April before I ever actually saw the pack in action. I was drowsing when they came but I woke up enough to try to fight back. There was a big black dog in the pack, and this shepherd-looking dog. That didn't look like any mongrel dog to me. It was marked with silver and black just like that dog your boy has. I winged the shepherd and thought I had killed it for sure, even though it dragged away into the woods fast. By the time I got the rest of them driven away and went to look for the shepherd, it was gone. I figured it had just made it back up into the hills to die."

Dad started to speak but Jordan didn't wait for him.

"After that I kept really careful watch at night. The next time they came I killed the black dog and there was no sign of the shepherd in the pack. It was peaceful then for the whole summer. I figured that I had either broken up the pack or they had found somebody else to steal from. That was it until last Thursday night. I had even quit staying out there. Instead, I bought a guard dog and felt pretty secure. That was a mistake because Thursday the whole pack came."

"And you saw them?" Dad asked.

Jordan Aggers nodded. "I was hammering away at some stalls in the barn when Ma came in hollering that dogs was at the lambs again.

"If I had had my gun I might have shot

two or three of them. As it was, I yelled for Ma to go after it while I tried to close in on them with a piece of stove wood in my hand. The rest of them run off but this one big German, he was gripping my guard dog and shaking the life out of him. When I went for him, the German let go of my dog and stood me off.

"It was a real shock to see him, I was that sure I had killed him that time before," Jordan went on. "But there he was, bigger and stronger than he had looked that first time. There was no way I could get near enough with only that stove wood but I kept threatening and he finally turned and took off, leaving my dog half dead and five lambs besides."

Jordan looked up at my dad but this time it was my dad who waited.

"Ma called Doc Fletcher. He had to wait a spell before coming and Ma and I tore sheets and took care of the animals best we could until he got there.

"It was while he was sewing up our dog that he told us about sewing up that dog of yours not ten minutes before."

It was clear that nobody was going to

break that silence but me. The room was so full of eyes that my throat nearly swelled shut.

My dad prodded me. "Miles?"

"Mister Wolf fought a groundhog," I told him, my voice sounding weak and funny. "We were out on Pin Hill gathering nuts when he got into a fight with this big groundhog."

"Doc Fletcher said he never saw wounds like that on such a big dog from any varmint," Jordan Aggers challenged.

"It was the biggest one I ever saw, Dad, with long yellow teeth and claws like talons."

"Did you save the carcass?" Dad asked quietly.

Sheriff Cravens cleared his throat and crossed his legs the other way. "We went out there in the rain today," he said, "Miles and me. We found a clearing that showed there had been a fight of some kind. There was even blood on the grass and Miles found a stick he said he used to pry the animals apart. But there wasn't any carcass there."

"I'm not out to make trouble for your boy or you," Jordan Aggers said to Dad. "But Ma hasn't got a thing in this world but me and that little parcel of stony ground out there. The first time I saw that kid's dog I was struck by how much it was marked like the shepherd I shot out at my place. When I saw the dog Thursday night again, I knew it was the same dog with no mistake."

"But Mister Wolf was with me all the time," I said desperately.

"Can you describe the dog you drove away from your dog and the flock?" Dad asked.

Jordan Aggers nodded firmly. "He's big and looks purebred. He's got that black-and-silvery coat, none of that tan and brownish look a lot of those dogs have."

Dad looked straight at me. "Call Mister Wolf," he said firmly.

I started to get up but Dad motioned me back. "Just call him," he repeated.

I called and whistled and we could all hear the laborious struggle Mister Wolf made getting to his feet. "Come on, boy, come on," I coaxed.

We heard his uneven progress along the hall and then he was standing in the door-way. He was carrying his head low from the pain of the stitches and his ears were down. Maybe if you didn't know him like I did, you might have thought he even looked mean. But the lamplight gleamed on that sleek sable-and-silver coat of his as he looked questioningly at me before crossing the room to lay his head on my knee.

Jordan Aggers nodded. "That's him," he said firmly. "That's the same dog, without a shadow of a doubt."

Chapter Seven

HOUSE ARREST

NOBODY SAID anything for a long minute. Then I heard Sheriff Cravens breathe out heavily and the creak of his chair as he stirred.

"What time would you say that you broke up that dog fight out in your sheep pen?" Dad asked Jordan Aggers.

"Between four-thirty and five-thirty, sometime," Jordan replied.

Dad turned to me. "And what time did you say you and Mister Wolf were out on Pin Hill?"

It almost choked me to have to repeat Jordan Agger's words but it was the closest I knew. "It must have been between four-

75

thirty and five," I said. "It was right up six when Mister Wolf and I got down to the common. At least I thought so because the lights were coming on by that time."

Dad shook his head. "That's a pretty tight time frame. What do you think we should do, Miles?"

"There's nothing to do," I told him. "It wasn't Mister Wolf who killed those sheep. He was with me all the time. It couldn't have been Mister Wolf."

"Yet Jordan here says it was Mister Wolf 'without the shadow of a doubt.' There's no way that you can *both* be right. What do *you* think we should do, Jordan?"

The young man twisted in his chair and put up a really good show of not liking to say what he did, but he didn't fool me. I just didn't realize that his words were going to hit me that hard.

"I think the dog should be done away with and the sooner the better for all concerned."

"No!" I shouted. "You can't do that. How come you think you can come in here and have my dog killed just because you lost a mess of nasty little sheep? You've no right!"

I could tell from the way Dad leaned forward that he was about to rebuke me but he never got the chance. It was Jordan Aggers who answered me, his face suddenly redder with fury.

"Because I've got nothing to lose by lying, kid, and you can't say the same. You got everything to gain by lying your way out of this. Killing your dog isn't going to bring back any dead sheep, it will only keep there from being any more. But you . . . if you get away with this, your dog gets off scot-free to kill again. If he was my dog I'd fight for him too. But I'd sure manage to come up with a better story than a giant-sized groundhog whose body disappears into thin air."

Without meaning to I had tightened my grip on Mister Wolf's ruff. He whimpered softly in complaint.

"Dad," I pleaded, "he can't do that. He can't just come in here and take away Mister Wolf on only his own say-so."

"I don't honestly know what anyone can do," Dad said quietly. "Maybe you can tell us the law on this, Jim."

Sheriff Cravens didn't look up as he answered Dad.

"An animal can be impounded on a signed complaint by a citizen who has sustained injury or damage to his property, like the sheep in this case. He can't be"—he struggled for a phrase and ended up using the same one that Jordan Aggers had— " 'done away with' without an order from a local magistrate who has weighed both sides of the question."

"Then that's what I'll get," Jordan Aggers said. He rose as if it was all settled and he was ready to leave.

"There's no way to hold a hearing on this until Monday," Sheriff Cravens reminded him.

"But he can be impounded," Jordan reminded him.

"On a written complaint," the sheriff agreed.

"Then you give me the form and I'll sign it right now and we'll get that animal put away."

"Where would he be impounded?" Dad asked, as if he had already given up and was ready to do anything they said.

"Those cages out there on Nickers' farm" Sheriff Cravens said apologetically. "That's all the facility the town has."

"But those are only cages," I protested. "They don't even have roofs on them to keep out the rain. The wind blows right through them and there are fleas and ticks and everything else left from other dogs . . . diseases even, probably. Mister Wolf is sick. He just had all those stitches. He'd die out there in the rain and the wind like that."

"We're only talking about from tonight to Monday," Jordan Aggers said in that disgusted voice that suggested that I was a whimpering baby or something.

"I don't know what else we can do, Miles," Dad told me.

"I do," I said quickly. "We can keep him here like he was on probation or something. We would promise to keep him on his lead all the time he was outside. It's not like he felt good enough to run around, anyway. He's sick. You'd agree to that, wouldn't you?" I asked Jordan Aggers.

"You have to be kidding," Jordan Aggers told me curtly. "I'm through fooling around. I really mean business now. I want that dog behind bars, preferably in the care of someone who knows how important 'a mess of

79

nasty little sheep' can be to a fellow making a living. Nickers is a farmer, too. He sounds fine to me."

I felt myself flush but I knew I had asked for that one. When nobody said anything, he went on angrily, "That dog has got to be impounded regular. You said that yourself, Sheriff. If there is a complaint against the dog he has to be impounded. There's no reason for any special treatment for this kid. Just because I'm who I am and he's what he is doesn't mean that his dog should get fancy service. I sure didn't come back to this snobbish little jerkwater town because I wanted to. I came to help Ma out. I know this town. If this was the other way around you'd be quick enough to slam a dog of mine out there in Nickers' field and let him rot. It's already high time this kid learns how it feels on the other side of the street. The dog goes to the pound. The law is with me."

I saw the look of shock on Dad's face being replaced by a kind of sad thoughtfulness. Then he turned to Sheriff Cravens. "We aren't asking for special privileges for Mister Wolf because of who we are. It's simply a matter of being humane to an injured animal."

"Very pretty," Jordan Aggers said. He was still on his feet, pressing and re-pressing his wet jacket with the flat of his hand. "Can we take the dog with us now, Sheriff? I'll sign the papers down at your office."

Sheriff Cravens remained solidly in his chair. "Now let's not rush this along, Jordan. I need to tell you one more thing about law in this township. That writ of complaint against an animal can only be executed if the law officer in the case feels that there is sufficient evidence to justify it. If I acted on every complaint one citizen wanted to sign against another one, there are people around here who would have to have their mail sent down to the jail."

I wondered if he was thinking about old Mr. Perkins and his brother-in-law when he said that.

"I've been listening to all this very carefully," he continued slowly, "trying to get a feel for what's fair to everyone concerned. There are still some unanswered questions in my mind." Then he turned to Dad. "Would you ask your wife to come back in here for a minute?"

Mom stood by Dad's chair, obviously confused as to why she had been sent for.

81

"I just have a few questions I want to ask," Sheriff Cravens explained. "Tell me exactly what happened Thursday."

She looked startled. "All day Thursday?" she asked.

He laughed and shook his head. "Just about the beginning of this nut-gathering business."

"Oh. That started Monday," she said. "I sort of hinted to Miles that the hickory nuts would be ready and he should go gather some. He didn't want to go. Then on Tuesday when I suggested it again, he had some other excuse."

Dad was grinning. "And Wednesday?" the sheriff asked.

"As I remember he was afraid to go because a storm was coming up that day," Mom explained dryly.

Everybody but Jordan Aggers and me looked pretty amused at that.

"Then what about Thursday?" he asked.

Mom's jaw came up the way it does when she shifts into high gear. "Let's just say that when Miles got off the bus he was ready to go nutting. I had packed brownies for him to eat on the way and had the nut-gathering bag ready for him to start out."

"Could you describe that nut-gathering bag?"

"Oh, sure," she said. "We always use the same one. It's sort of a homespun mesh and it has STONE GROUND stenciled on it in brown letters. It's from a mill where I used to buy whole wheat flour up in New Hampshire. That was before Miles got big enough to refuse anything with whole wheat in it."

"Can you show me that bag?" Sheriff Cravens asked.

She looked startled and shook her head. "I haven't seen it since Miles took it off with him on Thursday. I didn't think about it after he called from Doc Fletcher's, with Mister Wolf so torn up and all."

"But you would know the bag if you saw it?"

"Oh, in a minute," she said.

Sheriff Cravens heaved himself to his feet and went out to the front door where he had hung his jacket on the hall tree. When he came back, he handed Mom that bag I had taken to the woods. It was wet and had water streaks and was still half full of hickory nuts. "Is this the same one?" he asked.

She nodded and took the bag silently.

When Sheriff Cravens looked over at Jordan Aggers, his face was kind of sad. "Listen, Jordan. Try to be fair to the boy and the rest of us here in town. I went out to that clearing in Pin Hill with Miles today trying to get to the truth. When I looked at that clearing it was plain that some kind of a tussle had gone on there. Now maybe a half-grown kid would think to falsify evidence like that but I really doubt it. There was a club there like he told me he used and there was blood on the matted leaves on the clearing floor. Those things would be pretty hard for him to think to do if he was making up a big fancy lie to cover his dog's guilt. But he didn't even think about this bag of nuts. I just happened to spot it lying off in the woods a ways and went to see what it was. There's not a single hole in Miles's story that I can see. You say there's not a shadow of a doubt about Mister Wolf's being the sheep killer . . .

"I say I have more reason to believe Miles than I do to doubt him. On that basis, I can't see putting an injured dog out in October weather in an open cage. I'm putting him here under Miles's dad's supervision in what we can call 'house arrest.' "

Jordan Aggers' face was tight with fury as he turned to me. "Okay, kid, you win this round. But you better pray that nobody comes around my flock while you're baby-ing that sheep killer. I don't intend to be caught without a gun out there even one more time." He turned on his heel and strode swiftly to the door. "I'll be outside when you're ready to go have that complaint signed," he told Sheriff Cravens.

When I slam that door that hard I have to go back and shut it correctly with Mom standing over me. Dad and Sheriff Cravens exchanged a funny, sad look.

"He didn't have an easy growing-up, that boy," Sheriff Cravens reminded Dad, almost like an apology. "He's shifted the blame for that around in his mind a little, I'd say."

"It's probably easier for him," Dad agreed. "Now that old Aggers is dead and all."

Chapter Eight

A STAB IN THE BACK

WHEN I FIRST brought Mister Wolf home from the woods he was really nervous for a little puppy. He would only go to sleep in dark, hidden places. If you caught him off guard, he was very ferocious, baring his little milk teeth and threatening you with a terrible baby growl.

Actually, his readiness to take on any unexpected enemy was what earned him his name. While I was still making lists of names and trying to decide which one suited him best, he and Mom had their first tug-of-war.

She didn't know he was curled up asleep under the skirt of her chair by the fireplace.

She was whacking around there with the hearth broom and must have poked him. He grabbed the hearth broom and hung on. Mom thought the broom was snagged on something so she gave it a real hard tug. Out it came with that puppy hanging on like a turtle waiting for thunder. When the force of the tug shook him loose, he went flying across the room in a furry ball. But the minute he got his balance he roared back over there and attacked that broom as if it were his deadly enemy.

Mom yelled at me to come see. There he was, with legs all of four inches long and that soft wet baby nose but he was after that broom like the Great Fang of the North.

"All right, Mister Wolf," she laughed and laid the broom down where he could reach it. He grabbed one end of it and shook it all over the room until the rug looked like a straw bin and he was convinced that the broom was dead.

Then he laid both paws on it to guard it.

Somehow no name ever sounded right after that, and Mister Wolf he became.

Right from the beginning he got to sleep in my room. Mom even put an old beach towel down in the corner behind my bed so he would have his special place.

That night I lay and listened to his even breathing from the darkness in the corner. I tried not to think of what might happen Monday when Jordan Aggers would go before the magistrate. I even hoped that whoever heard the complaint would be somebody who knew his bad reputation from before and wouldn't believe him now. I knew how lucky I was Sheriff Cravens was such a fair man, or right then Mister Wolf would have been out there shivering in the wind at Nickers' farm.

Monday seemed awfully close. What if we ran away, Mister Wolf and me? Could we get far enough to be safe from Jordan Aggers? Other kids ran away. Jordan Aggers himself had done it. Hadn't Mr. Austen told me that he had taken off from home without even finishing high school? The only trouble was that running away would make Mister Wolf look guilty when he wasn't. And then there were Mom and Dad.

The wind rose and filled my room with strange night sounds. I kept imagining that I heard the howl of the wild dog pack and

it made my throat ache so that I put the pillow on top of my head instead of underneath.

Mom is always talking about how hard Dad works all week but I personally think he spends most of his time thinking up jobs for Saturday. That Saturday it was firewood. I wanted to take Mister Wolf back into the woods where Dad had felled a tree but Dad shook his head.

"We can fasten him to a tree real securely and he can enjoy the nice fresh air while we work," I coaxed.

Dad shook his head. "If he tugged loose, where would you be?" he asked. "He can stay in the house and be warm. Every time you take a cart full of wood back to the bin you can stop and go pet him."

Dad and I got five carts of wood hauled in before Mom called us to lunch. Then Mister Wolf and I took a long, long walk in our own woods. I sat on a stone fence for a long time and watched the way he checked the smells on the wind and listened to the secret things moving in the brush about us. You could tell how much better he was feeling by the way he perked those ears up at the smallest new sound from anywhere. The only thing bad was the raw, hairless place under his chin where Doc Fletcher had put in all those stitches. But you couldn't even see that unless he had his head lifted up into the wind.

We'd been out there quite a long time when I heard Dad calling me. Mister Wolf didn't feel much like running so I yelled to Dad and we took our time getting back to the house.

I saw that there were two men standing with Dad the minute we got to the edge of the back yard. It was Sheriff Cravens again, and Dad's friend Mr. Austen was with him. I decided it wouldn't hurt Mister Wolf to run just that little way across the lawn.

"What's up?" I asked Dad as soon as I got close. He and Sheriff Cravens both looked a little too serious to be reassuring.

"Well," Sheriff Cravens began. "Things have changed a little about your dog there."

"Changed?" I asked. "He hasn't been out of our sight."

"I believe that, Miles," he nodded. "But Mr. Austen here . . ." The sheriff's voice stopped.

Mr. Austen here looked like a kid with his fist in the jam jar. He was sweating in spite of the coolness of the day and he changed his weight from one foot to another as Sheriff Cravens spoke his name.

"I'm sorry, Miles," Mr. Austen blurted out. "I really fought with myself about this and decided that I had to do what I had to do."

"What are you talking about?" I asked, half scared at seeing a grown-up man sweat like that.

"Well, you know how talk gets around in this town?"

It was like an appeal and when I nodded, he went on.

"I was up at Leominister all day yesterday and didn't hear about what you and Jordan Aggers were into over your dog. But you know my wife, Millie, works over at the library and she heard all about it more than once. It was Millie who reminded me how I had come home Thursday night still trembling from thinking I almost hit a dog out on the north end of town.

"I had described the whole thing to her. How I was driving along and this big dog

93

seemed to appear out of nowhere, with his skin hanging and his jowls all covered with blood and the wildest kind of look in his eyes. I even mentioned to her that although I was sure I was wrong, the dog I caught out there in my headlights looked exactly like your Mister Wolf."

He stopped and just stared at me.

"I fretted it all night, Miles. I've never had more than just reports of mischief on you but I remember that Aggers kid as a real terror. But right is right. I'm sorry but I felt it was my duty to tell the sheriff here about seeing your dog all bloodied out there near the Aggers' place."

"It *was* Mister Wolf," I told him quickly. "I was right up there on the slope behind him trying to get through that barbed-wire fence. I even yelled at the car hoping who-ever it was would give us a ride back to town."

"Way out there, Miles?" Sheriff Cravens asked mildly. "I asked Austen here to show me on the township map where he saw the dog. He pointed to a spot a quarter of a mile north of the clearing we went to on Pin Hill."

"It was getting dark in the woods," I protested. "I was trying to get back to the north-south road any way I could so I wouldn't lose my way out there. I might have cut north without knowing it. I was only thinking of working east to connect with the road."

"That makes some sense, Miles, but not quite enough. The dog had been injured and you were making him walk maybe an extra mile or two."

"Even if I took the risk of getting lost?" I protested. I was beginning to get scared all over again. And mad. I always thought Mr. Austen was my friend. I knew he had been Dad's friend ever since I could remember. Why, he and his wife came over to our house for barbecues and everything. Yet here he was going out of his way to take that stranger's side against one of his own townspeople.

And even Dad. He hadn't said a single word since Mister Wolf and I crossed that lawn. He was just looking at me and waiting.

"Dad," I pleaded. "Mister Wolf was with me. He fought the groundhog and he was with me all the time. Anything but that is a dirty rotten lie."

"It was your word against Jordan Aggers'

until now, Miles," he pointed out quietly. "But can't you see that this new development changes it a little bit?"

"You mean you're going to let them take Mister Wolf out there to Nickers' farm?"

Dad shook his head. "We talked that over while we were waiting for you. Sheriff Cravens has agreed that if Dr. Fletcher will put him up in his kennels behind the office that it will constitute a proper impoundment. There's a storm warning out for tonight. Someone will be at the office and we'll all feel better about the dog."

"But the money for his board . . . ," I began, thinking of how much Dad had complained about all the vet bills we had when Mister Wolf was just a pup, for the shots and the infected tick that the doctor had to dig out, and then the time he had pushed over the beehive and had to take shots to get the swelling down from that.

"I can't think of anything less important to me right now than Mister Wolf's board bill." Dad's voice sounded really tired all of a sudden. "Why don't you go in and bring Mister Wolf's blanket out here so he'll feel more at home in that strange place?"

"I wish I had run away last night when I thought about it," I told him. "I wish I had taken Mister Wolf and run away before you decided to believe that Jordan Aggers instead of me! You all just don't even care that he's going to have him killed . . ."

Dad broke in quietly. "Go get the rug, Miles," he said flatly.

I went and got the rug and a handful of biscuits and a piece of rawhide that Mister Wolf liked to chew on. I wasn't going to break down in front of them. They could all turn against me, Dad, Sheriff Cravens and that bigmouthed Mr. Austen but I wouldn't give them the satisfaction of letting them see me cry.

But that ache that comes in the back of my throat and makes my eyes water came anyway so I kept my face away from them all. I stroked Mister Wolf just a minute down the long glossy length of his back and patted him on the rump. He looked up at me and smiled that way with his tongue out at the side.

"Take care, fellow," I said and turned around and went back into the house so I wouldn't have to see them take him away.

Everything went crazy from that minute on. It was like I was boiling inside and there wasn't even anybody I could yell at.

I can always depend on Mom to stand right up to me and give me as good as I put out. It's a kind of a game we've worked out over the years. I insult her and she insults me and the one with the best line wins. We never have any of that sloppy stuff you see between some kids and their moms. So what did Mom do when I needed her the very most?

You guessed. She turned sweet and gentle on me. Every time I caught her eyes they looked soft and moist like ripe fruit that had been stepped on. I couldn't stand it. I went upstairs and closed the door to my room.

Later I heard the phone ring but I didn't pay any attention. When Dad called me I yelled down that I didn't want to talk to anyone. Would you believe—he just called back up to me and said, "Take your call on the phone in our bedroom."

I sat there a few minutes before I could make myself pick up the phone. It was Matt Turpin and his voice sounded strange and sort of embarrassed.

"I heard about your dog," he said. "That's rotten."

"Sure," I said.

"You're still going out with us tonight, aren't you?" he asked.

"Out where?" I asked.

"Fry that," he said disgustedly. "Out for trick or treat—what else on Hallowe'en?"

Hallowe'en. How could I have forgotten it was Hallowe'en? I felt like an old, old man who loses track of whole hunks of time from soft places in the head.

"I'm checking out," I told him. "Try me some other year."

"Hey, come on, Miles," he coaxed. "We have some new ideas that you won't believe this year." I heard some whispering behind him and his voice *shush*ing the other guys. "We got one idea that you'll really dig but I'm afraid to tell it over the phone."

"Not this time," I said. "Have fun anyway." And I hung up. Then I realized that I hadn't heard that click that comes when they hang up the downstairs phone. So maybe the way things were going I could expect even my own dad and mom to spy on me.

It was maybe an hour later that Dad came to my door and rapped. I answered and he stood there a minute. I never did ask him to come in but he did anyway.

"Are you going out with your friends tonight?" he asked.

I shook my head. "You must have heard me tell them on the phone."

He flushed. "Thanks, Miles," he said dryly. Then he made a visible effort to look brighter. "Mom and I thought if you weren't going out, the three of us could go over to the Inn in Concord and have dinner."

I shook my head. "You go on. I'm not hungry."

"None of us are hungry, Miles," he pointed out. "So we'll all go out and not eat dinner together. That will at least take some of the weight off your mom, if it doesn't do anything else."

That's the kind of thing he says when he wants me to feel worse but it didn't work that time. Right then I was sure that there wasn't any way in the world I could possibly feel worse. Ever.

Chapter Nine

CARNAGE

BY THE TIME we got home from Concord that Saturday night all the little kids were already off the streets. We saw some bunches of older kids prowling around with big sacks to beg candy from any house stupid enough to have left a lit jack-o'-lantern out front. Seeing them with their ape masks and their hobo outfits reminded me of Matt Turpin and the guys. I wondered passingly what special trick they had thought up that Matt was afraid to tell me over the phone. The dullness in my chest about Mister Wolf kept me from being interested enough to check it out with anyone.

Those guys were probably not even home

yet when I went to bed. It was a fight to go to sleep in that room whose silence seemed eerie without Mister Wolf's steady, even breathing from the dark beside my bed.

Mom laid a folded blanket at my feet, saying that I might need it for the coming storm. Actually, I figured she was just trying to tell me she was thinking about me and didn't know any other way short of getting sloppy.

But she was right about the storm. I was wakened by that funny tapping from the shutters of their room. When I got up to unfold the blanket I saw that the strange lightness outside was from falling snow.

It wasn't the heaviest fall I ever saw but it was definitely snow, piling against the bases of the bushes in the yard and pasting itself against the trunks of the trees. I thought about Mister Wolf. He was too young to remember another winter, so snow would be something new to him. What if he wasn't even going to be around to snap and jump at snow like I have seen other puppies do? Just thinking about it made it hard to go back to sleep, and then, before it was even full dawn, I was wakened again by the sound of men's voices.

I stiffened to listen, trying to figure out who would be downstairs talking to Dad at the crack of dawn on Sunday morning.

I was already out on the floor when Dad opened my door very cautiously.

"Sheriff Cravens is here, Miles," he whispered. "He wants us to take a little trip with him."

"What for?" I asked. "What's it all about?"

"Just dress warmly," he cautioned, still in that very careful voice. "And don't forget boots."

From the way he was whispering I figured that Mom must still be asleep. As I tiptoed past their room I could see that untidy mop of dark curls on the far pillow and knew I was right. I hesitated in the hall a minute, hoping she would open her eyes and see me there. That was silly. I tiptoed on downstairs with my boots in my hand.

Dad had scribbled something on a half sheet of notebook paper. He was putting it under a magnet on the refrigerator when I came into the kitchen.

"In case your mom wakes up before we get back," he explained.

His expression was so strange that I read the note while I tied the laces at the tops of my boots. It didn't tell me anything. It only said that he and I were gone and would be back soon. Lots to learn from that, I thought as I followed Dad out and got into the back of Sheriff Craven's car.

Not until we passed the common and started out the road going north did it occur to me that we might be headed for Jordan Aggers' place, but that didn't make any sense. It would have scared me except that I could picture Mister Wolf safe in one of those cages at Doc Fletcher's, pacing back and forth and watching the snow come down.

The men hardly talked at all.

"Pretty heavy for a first snow," Dad said.

"It'll never stick on," Sheriff Cravens replied. "The ground's still too warm."

When they turned off onto the old Post Road I was as sure as anything that we were headed for Aggers' even if it still didn't make any sense. Because that road isn't as important as it was back in the old days and they don't keep it up very well. Sheriff Cravens slowed down to maneuver the ruts that caught at his wheels. Every once in a while I saw a white circle where snow had completely filled a pothole. We passed the old Post Inn all boarded up and I could see the long and short of rabbit tracks crisscrossing the front drive.

Then I heard the drumming.

For years my friends and I have biked out there and listened by the hour, hoping to hear that ghostly sound. We never heard even the first tap. Yet there, over the sound of the car's motor, I heard the slow cadence begin, then increase speed to a frantic pace and then stop suddenly, like halfway through a breath, like your own breath does when you are really startled.

Superstition, I told myself. The whole Ghostly Drummer story was trumped up by somebody to scare people. A fellow could probably even figure out what caused that noise if he really wanted to look into it. But I wasn't able to think very clearly right then. Being hauled out of bed and taken off into the night was enough to spook me, without hearing that strange steady rapping muffled by snow. I listened numbly, remembering how people said that to hear the sound of the Ghostly Drummer was a really bad omen. They said it always meant that something really ugly was going to happen to you.

And neither Dad nor Sheriff Cravens showed a sign of hearing a thing!

I never saw the Aggers' farm until we pulled up that rutted lane, but right off it looked the way Jordan Aggers did, mean and poor and hunched in. The house was a tall, thin two-story frame that looked as if it had never seen paint. A cluster of rusty farm machinery huddled out by the barn, and dead vegetation was snagging the snow in rows of what must have been a summer garden. One window in the house gleamed light as we pulled into the drive, but Jordan Aggers was out by the fence waiting for us.

He must have been standing there just like that for a long time. One side of his clothing had turned white from the blowing snow so that he looked rooted, as if he couldn't have walked away if he wanted to.

Nobody said anything. Jordan Aggers didn't even glance at me. Instead, when we came even with the fence, he opened the gate and held it while we walked through. Then he neatly latched it behind us. We passed the barn and a smelly chicken house

106

where a cock was screaming morning and some hens were clucking crossly back at him. Then we got to the corner of the next building and Jordan Aggers stopped.

When I am about one hundred years old and have been everywhere in the world and have seen everything in the world I expect maybe I can get that picture out of my mind. Anyway I hope so.

The smell hit first, an oily kind of smell with some sick, sweet odor mixed in. We were facing a big fenced-in area and the ground everywhere was splashed with scarlet on that snow. It was blood, blood everywhere. There on the white, like toys that some kid had torn apart and thrown away, were dead lambs. They had been split open and dragged around the yard so that great streaks of red showed against the white. Their necks were at odd, broken angles and their eyes stared steadily off at nothing. The only old dead sheep was huge with yellowed curly hair and great horns, but he was broken and thrown away just like the little ones. The rest of the sheep were clustered against the fence, staring at us with wide, expressionless eyes.

My stomach began to grab at itself, kind of like cramps. Then I got hiccoughs, not ordinary hiccoughs but deep, quick hiccoughs that brought the food up from my stomach. I stood there vomiting and didn't even know it was coming. Dad must have handed me his handkerchief because later I realized I had it in my hand.

Right then, in the middle of my being so sick, one of the female sheep separated herself from the group by the fence and crossed the yard. She walked in small, neat steps like a lady on an urgent social errand. She went straight to one of the dead lambs and sniffed at it. She nudged it a few times with her nose as if to try to make it get up. Then she raised her head to the sky and began to cry. Her tongue looked fat and pink and curled, with the snow landing on it as she mourned in that rough choppy rhythm of a sheep's cry.

Jordan Aggers seemed like some other guy. All the anger and resentment had gone from him and he seemed old. A tired patience heavied his voice as he spoke.

"That enough?" he asked quietly.

When my dad nodded, Jordan turned and

walked into the shelter that ran alongside the sheepyard. Just inside the shelter he leaned over and tugged a big green tarp up and threw it off onto the snowy ground.

I felt like somebody had hit me in my stomach. My lungs wouldn't work at all. A flood ran out of my eyes and burnt going down my cheeks, but I couldn't have said a word if my life depended on it.

There on the floor of that sheep shelter, with his delicate legs crossed at the ankle the way he always sleeps, lay Mister Wolf. His head was down on his chest so that the fine black arch of the back of his neck was a graceful curve. There couldn't be any mistake. Every line of silver and tuft of glossy black hair was the same. He looked beautiful and peaceful and absolutely still as his open eyes stared past the gaping bullet hole in the middle of his forehead.

I saw Jordan Aggers' face begin to rotate slowly as his eyes met mine; then I saw the ground of the sheep enclosure start to move upward unevenly, bearing the fuzzy images of the dead sheep into the air with it. Something caught hard at my elbow and I heard Dad's voice say, as if from a long way away,

"Hang on, Miles. Hang on." Then I don't remember anything more about that place.

It still makes me feel really silly that I checked out like that. It's embarrassing to realize that those three men had to pick me up like a baby and stow me in the back seat of Sheriff Craven's car. When I started coming to, it was with a slow, sickening rhythm in my head that carried their voices.

"Maybe it was too strong medicine," Sheriff Cravens was saying. "But I couldn't argue with Jordan that he needed to see this for himself to believe it. What other way was there to make him understand?"

"None," Dad said quietly. "He's not a kid, not at thirteen. I wouldn't have believed it myself." His voice kind of trailed off.

It was Jordan Aggers' voice that brought me all the way awake. Like I said, there wasn't any anger left in the man. His voice sounded flat and tired and hurt. "You'll have to take my word that I'm sorry. But you know I had no choice. It's easy to get ticked off by a cocky kid like that and I admit he got to me a couple of times. He sure stuck by that animal the whole way, you have to give him that."

111

I lay perfectly still until I felt the vibration of the engine start and the car bumping along the rough lane that led back down to the old Post Road. Then I heard the rustle as Dad turned from the front seat.

"How are you doing back there?" he asked softly.

"Okay, I guess," I replied.

"We had to let you see it for yourself," Sheriff Cravens said, like an apology.

I struggled up in the seat. "But I don't understand," I protested. "How did he ever get out of Doc Fletcher's? I thought he was safe in there."

"We all did." Sheriff Cravens voice was rueful. "It was somebody's idea of a Hallowe'en prank. They cut open all the pens over at Fletcher's last night. By the time the attendant heard the noise, there was only one animal left, a toy French poodle standing in his water dish, barking bloody murder."

Chapter Ten

THE UNRAVELING

IT WASN'T THAT I wanted to die, it was more that I couldn't imagine how it would be to live any more. Mister Wolf hadn't been my first pet—we had a really prickly cat once when I was little that stayed until I was crazy about him and then just walked away. I had been through gerbils and guinea pigs too, and even a white rat which Mom never would have permitted except for my ruptured appendix.

But Mister Wolf was different. Mister Wolf was like the other half of me. While I was teaching him, he kind of taught me too. We understood each other, or I thought I understood him until I saw him out there at Jordan Aggers' like that.

113

The car was even quieter going back home than it had been on our trip out there. When Sheriff Cravens pulled up in our driveway, Dad asked him to come in and have some coffee and warm himself up.

The sheriff just shook his head. "I don't think you need me around here today."

Dad nodded and leaned against the sheriff's side of the car. "Thanks for doing all you could for us, Jim." Then he turned to me. "How about you, Miles?"

I nodded and Sheriff Cravens looked at me searchingly.

"Anything you want to tell me, son?"

What was there to tell him? That I knew who had turned those animals loose at Fletcher's the night before, because I was pretty sure I did? Or that I had been lying all the time about the groundhog and was ready to admit that Mister Wolf was a bad dog from the start?

"You wouldn't want to hear it," I told him.

"Try me," he said.

"Mister Wolf was cut up by a groundhog on Thursday," I said stubbornly. "No matter how come he was out there last night, he was with me on Thursday afternoon."

Mom had opened the storm door and was

waving out at us. She had on that rose-colored housecoat with the pocket that always hangs down because she catches it on doorknobs. She kept waving until Sheriff Cravens waved back and then she waved even harder.

"What do you suppose is on her mind?" Dad asked. He started up the walk while I watched Sheriff Cravens turn his car around in the drive to be ready to pull out. When he got to the door and spoke to Mom, Dad turned around and waved too, and yelled something I couldn't hear over the sound of the motor.

The sheriff frowned and rolled down the window so he could hear.

"What's up?" he shouted.

"Just kill your motor and come in," Dad yelled. He had a funny sound to his voice. "You too, Miles," he added. It must have looked silly to him the way I was just standing out there letting my clothes turn white with snow.

I saw him the minute I reached the door. I stopped so suddenly that Sheriff Cravens, right behind me, almost knocked me down.

Mom had put a beach towel on the

breakfast-room floor, pushing the table and chairs back against the wall to make room. It was weird the way he was lying there just the way that other dog had—everything, the angle of his ears, the way his legs were crossed at the ankle, the bright silver markings and the deep black of his coat. Only Mister Wolf had his head up so that you could see, down on the left side of his neck, that shaved off place where Doc Fletcher had sewed him up. His underbelly was matted with dirt and filth like he had come a long way and maybe even swum through mire to get there. His breath was deep and even in exhausted sleep.

"He woke me up scratching at the door," Mom explained. "How do you suppose he ever got away from the vet's? When I found your note I guessed you had heard he was out and gone to look for him. Poor fellow. He must have wanted to come home awfully bad."

The three of us stared at him so stupidly that her own face began to look fearful.

"What's wrong?" she asked breathlessly. Then she reached out and grabbed at my

117

jacket without taking her eyes from Dad's face. "There's nothing wrong," she decided out loud. "There is absolutely nothing wrong and you know it." Her voice was suddenly sharp and cross the way it gets when she is afraid.

The warmth of the kitchen with Mister Wolf lying there safely asleep plus the sound of Mom being herself were too much for me. I couldn't help it. I began to laugh.

"Nothing," I shouted, grabbing her. "Nothing in the whole wide world." When I took hold of her, some of the snaps on her housecoat popped open. She snatched at her clothes and darted an embarrassed glance at Sheriff Cravens.

"You quit mauling me, Miles Orten," she said crossly. "And clean that snow off your feet before you ruin my kitchen. Both of you," she added fiercely, glaring at Dad.

But we were all past being bullied by then. Dad looked at Sheriff Cravens and they both burst into laughter along with me. Dad took Mom by the shoulders. She couldn't fight him because she was still trying to get her snaps fastened up on that silly housecoat. Dad just backed her off gently into a chair.

"We have a long strange story to tell you," he said quietly. "And while Miles tells it, I'll make us some coffee."

She started up but he shook his head. "I was making coffee for Jim Cravens and me when you were still in junior high," he reminded her. "And that was over a campfire which is a lot harder than doing it here."

"I should think so," she said tartly. "The pot is already full and you know where the cups are."

The noise and confusion wakened Mister Wolf. I heard the slow easy thump of his tail, and he whimpered a little. I knelt down by him and stroked his head to assure him that everything was all right. His nose felt hot and dry to my touch and he smelled of the medicine that Dr. Fletcher had used on his wounds.

I don't know what had made Dad think I could tell Mom where we had been, and what we had seen. Sheriff Cravens knew I couldn't do it because he started in about Jordan Aggers' having called him a little after midnight.

"He wanted me to come out right then and bring Miles along. I persuaded him to wait until dawn at least."

"But why did you have to take him at all?" Her anger was gone and she sounded kind of sick as she took the mug of coffee Dad had poured for her. It was only then that I realized that here she was, truly wide awake, and it was only a little after seven.

"Jordan felt that Miles would be able to take Mister Wolf's death better if he saw why it *had* to happen."

"Are you trying to tell me that he put Miles through that awful experience out of kindness, a little boy like Miles?"

"Miles had taken on this fight like a man and he had stayed by Mister Wolf like a man. He deserved to take the punishment the same way," Dad told her.

"And as for Jordan being kind," Sheriff Cravens said quietly, "who knows what that boy is really like inside? Or how he would have been if he had been raised without an empty stomach and a horsewhip on his backside every time his dad hit the sauce?"

I was down on the beach towel with Mister Wolf's head up on my knee but I saw that soft look coming on Mom's face. Mister Wolf was alive and safe. The churning in my stomach had gone, leaving me only a sickly sour taste in my mouth. More than anything I wanted things back like they had been before that whole miserable thing had begun. And that included having Mom act like her same old feisty self again.

"I go hungry a lot of times myself," I said in a tone of mock bravery. "I can only stand it because I know that she has to feed me weekends when Dad is around."

Mom's mouth flew open and I expected a yell of protest, but then the corner of her mouth tucked down. "He's right," she said meekly. "I won't even buy liniment for the chain marks on his ankles, and I rub salt in the places where I pinch him with pliers."

Dad chuckled because it must have sounded like home to him too, but Sheriff Cravens wasn't even listening. He was blowing softly into his coffee mug and frowning at the ripples he made.

"Brothers," Sheriff Cravens said thoughtfully. "That's how it had to be, those two dogs must have been full brothers. I just wonder if there are any more out there somewhere."

Dad and I stared at him.

"It all fits together," he said quietly.

"Look back on what we know. We had almost enough clues to figure it out from the
first. Jordan shot a shepherd like this in late
April, thought he had killed it, but never
found the dead animal. He never said
whether it was a male or female because he
probably couldn't tell in the bad light and
the excitement of the fray. It had to be a
mother dog and she had to have made it
back to her cave and her litter. How old
would you say that pup was when you found
him, Miles?"

I shook my head. "Just little, he hardly
knew how to drink."

The sheriff nodded. "Weakened by the
shot and unable to hunt, she probably just
died later there in the cave with her pups.
If they were fast on their feet at all they
would have wandered off, like your Mister
Wolf did, looking for water and food—in-
sects and small game. That other dog *had* to
be a full brother. Why, he's the spit image of
Mister Wolf here."

"It still doesn't make sense to me," Mom
protested. "These aren't run-of-the-pack
dogs. Why would a purebred be out in those
woods wild in the first place? Who fathered

122

the pups? Mister Wolf and his brother had to have a father just like themselves to be so perfectly marked."

Sheriff Cravens shook his head. "You ought to get a look in my files to stop those questions. We get letters and calls and reward notices all the time for lost dogs. People sell dogs and the dogs go searching for their old masters. Animals wander away from campsites or jump out of cars in strange places. I'd bet somebody somewhere has a file that shows a bred shepherd missing early this year . . . say January or February. After a while people give up looking, knowing how dangerous the roads are for runaway pets."

"But the mother was wild," Mom insisted, "She was running with the pack and killing lambs just like the others."

"We call that 'feral,'" Sheriff Cravens said. "When a tame animal turns to the wild it is feral. A mother animal will find food for herself and her young with a desperation you wouldn't believe she had. You have to remember that dogs were wild animals a lot more centuries than they have been domesticated."

"Would Mister Wolf have been wild like that if I hadn't found him?" I asked, feeling a little sick at the thought.

"Sure as anything," he said. "He just lucked into it with you."

"Like I did with him," I stated proudly.

"I think you ought to be the one who gets to tell Jordan Aggers how this has all turned out," he added.

"Oh, I don't want to," I said quickly.

"Still have hard feelings against him?" the sheriff asked.

I shook my head. "It's more that I feel bad. It's like he said . . . I had everything to win and he had nothing but losing."

"I wouldn't quite buy that," Sheriff Cravens said. "He won a little yesterday and he was bright enough to realize it and fair enough to admit he was wrong."

"How can you say that?" My mind was suddenly full again of that awful scene in the sheep pen.

"Austen," the sheriff said briskly. "When Austen came forward of his own accord and stood by Aggers' story against yours, Aggers got a new insight into this 'jerkwater town.'"

"So did I," I admitted quietly, remembering how it felt when the weight of evidence
had turned against me.

"So what am I supposed to say to him?" I
asked when Dad handed me the phone.

"We have confidence in you, Miles," Mom
said in that half-kidding, sarcastic way of
hers. "You'll think of something!"

One thing about the people around our
house. They have all been brought up right
(if you'll excuse the immodesty). While I was
looking up the number in the book, Dad
refilled the coffee cups and suggested they
go try the new firewood that he and I had
brought in the day before.

By the time I dialed the number and
heard that broken country ring of the Aggers' phone, there was nobody in the
kitchen except Mister Wolf, who was asleep
again, and me.

When I finally hung up, I laid a dog biscuit
right down by Mister Wolf's nose in case he
waked up while I was in the other room.
Then I took a glass of milk in by the fire with
the others.

Mom angled her eyebrows at Dad.
"That's the fellow who is always ragging at

me about being long-winded on the phone."

"Jordan was telling me about growing up on that place out there," I explained. "And about how when he was a kid he got some really good clues to the mystery of that Ghostly Drummer."

Since nobody said anything and I could do without their wise, pleased looks, I rolled over on my stomach and stared into the fire.

"In fact"—it was really too exciting to keep to myself—"next spring when the ground clears, Jordan and Mister Wolf and me are going to track down some of those clues for ourselves."

At the mention of his name, Mister Wolf stirred from his sleep. We could all hear the slow, heavy thump of his tail on the kitchen floor. That lump came in the back of my throat again. Only different this time.

About the Author

MARY FRANCIS SHURA is the author of sixteen books for young people. Among the places in America where she and her husband and their four children have made their home is the area northwest of Boston where *Mister Wolf and Me* is set.

Aside from writing fiction for young readers and adults, Mary Francis Shura enjoys tennis, chess, reading, and cooking.

The author currently makes her home in the western suburbs of Chicago, in the village of Willowbrook.

About the Artist

KONRAD HACK also lives near Chicago, in Niles. He holds a Fine Arts degree from the University of Chicago, and he was a combat artist for the Department of Military History in Vietnam. His work is represented in the Society of Illustrators' book *200 Years of American Illustration*.